9379

DUNBA

P9-DCI-903

3 3495 00059131 6 E CAR
How to lose all your friends

DATE DUE

SEP 30 2003			
MAR 14 2006			

E
CAR

3 3495 00059131 6
Carlson, Nancy L.

How to lose all your friends

9379

DUNBAR SCHOOL LIBRARY
GLEN ELLEN, CA 95442

868590 01114 35803A 001

9379
DUNBAR SCHOOL LIBRARY
11700 DUNBAR ROAD
GLEN ELLEN, CALIFORNIA 95442

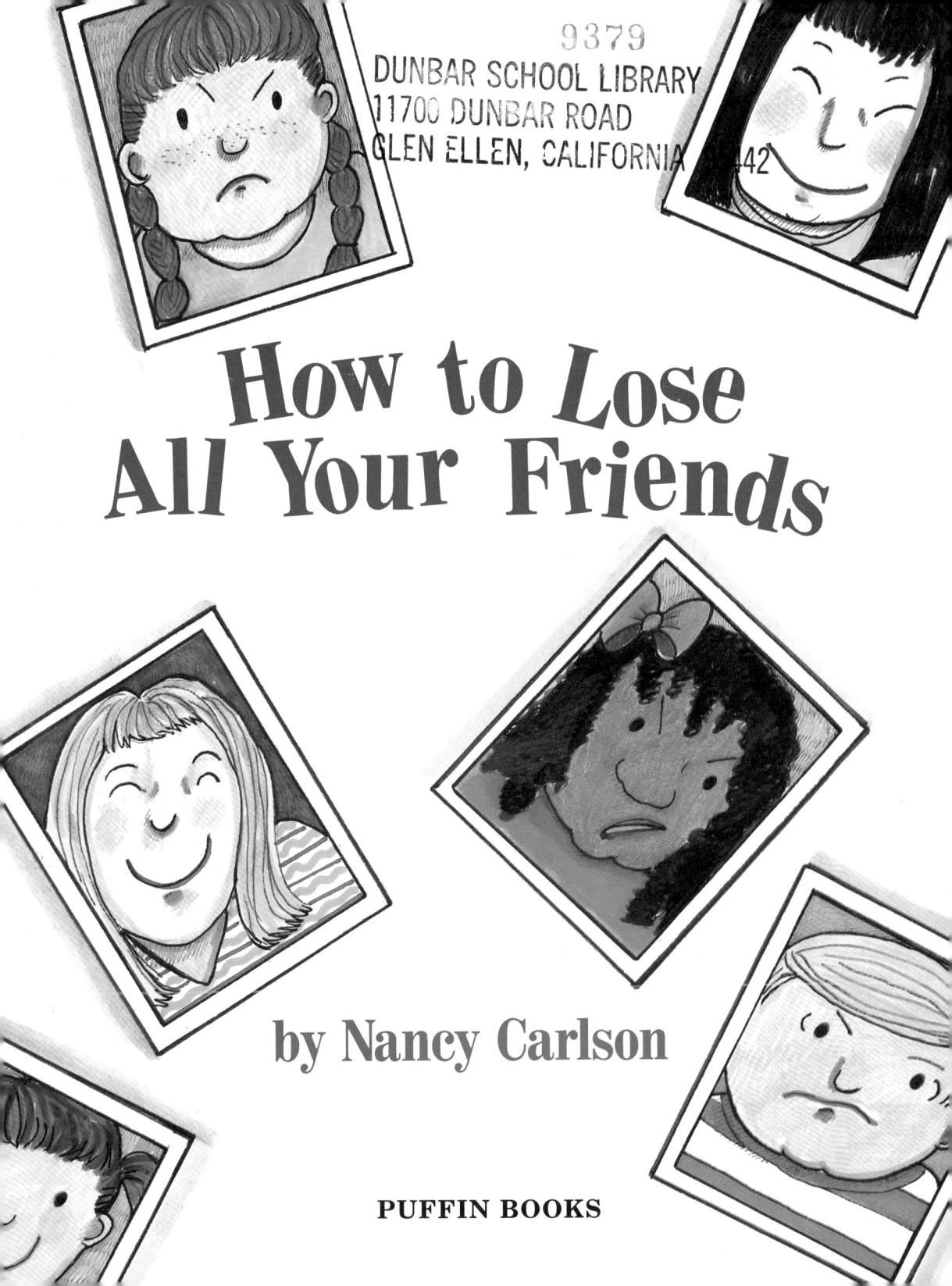

How to Lose All Your Friends

by Nancy Carlson

PUFFIN BOOKS

PUFFIN BOOKS
Published by the Penguin Group
Penguin Books USA Inc., 375 Hudson Street, New York, New York 10014, U.S.A.
Penguin Books Ltd, 27 Wrights Lane, London W8 5TZ, England
Penguin Books Australia Ltd, Ringwood, Victoria, Australia
Penguin Books Canada Ltd, 10 Alcorn Avenue, Toronto, Ontario, Canada M4V 3B2
Penguin Books (N.Z.) Ltd, 182-190 Wairau Road, Auckland 10, New Zealand
Penguin Books Ltd, Registered Offices: Harmondsworth, Middlesex, England

First published in the United States of America by Viking,
a division of Penguin Books USA Inc., 1994

Published in Puffin Books, 1997

3 5 7 9 10 8 6 4

Copyright © Nancy Carlson, 1994
All rights reserved

THE LIBRARY OF CONGRESS HAS CATALOGED THE VIKING EDITION AS FOLLOWS:

Carlson, Nancy L.
How to lose all your friends / by Nancy Carlson. p. cm.
Summary: Offers advice on the kinds of things to do
if you don't want to have any friends.
ISBN 0-670-84906-5
[1. Behavior—Fiction. 2. Friendship—Fiction.] I. Title.
PZ7.C21665Ho 1994 [E]—dc20 92-28368 CIP AC

Puffin Books ISBN 0-14-055862-4

Printed in the United States of America

Except in the United States of America, this book is sold subject to the condition that
it shall not, by way of trade or otherwise, be lent, re-sold, hired out, or otherwise
circulated without the publisher's prior consent in any form of binding or cover
other than that in which it is published and without a similar condition
including this condition being imposed on the subsequent purchaser.

For Kelly, Pat and Mike,
because sometimes
their mother is a crab!

If you don't want to have any friends,
follow these simple instructions:

1. Never smile

Be gloomy.

Be cranky.

Frown a lot.

Being gloomy and cranky, and frowning
will scare off any friends!

2. Never share

If you are eating cookies, hide them
when your friends come over.

You could also stuff them all in your mouth,
or you could just run away.

When you're playing with toys, grab
all the good ones for yourself.

Then throw a tantrum if somebody else
plays with one of them.

You can also just lock everyone
out of your bedroom.

3. Be a bully

Pick on little kids.

Push in front of the lunch line.

Play mean tricks on kids.

4. Be a poor sport

When you play tag and someone tags you,
lie, and say they missed.

Cheat at cards; if you're losing
a board game, knock off all the pieces.

5. Tattle

Tell on kids when they run in the hall.

When your brother makes a face at you, tell your mom. If your brother is in Time Out, make sure he stays there.

Now if you still have friends after all that,
I have one more lesson.

6. Whine!

Whine when it's too hot outside.
Whine when it's too cold outside.

Whine for treats.
That will irritate everyone.

If you follow these instructions you'll
be able to eat all the cookies you want.

And you will have no friends

to bother you.